W9-BIL-720

LIBRARY OF
MINNESOTA RENAISSANCE SOCIETY

LIBRARY OF
MINNESOTA RENAISSANCE SOC.

Adventures of HUCKLEBERRY FINN

The Young Collector's
Illustrated Classics

Adventures of
HUCKLEBERRY
FINN

By
Mark Twain

Adapted by
Suzanne McCabe

Illustrated by
Richard Lauter

Cover art by Richard Lauter

Copyright © 1999 Masterwork Books
A Division of Kidsbooks, Inc.
3535 West Peterson Avenue
Chicago, IL 60659

All rights reserved including the right of
reproduction in whole or in part in any form.

Manufactured in the United States of America

*Visit us at* www.kidsbooks.com
Volume discounts available for group purchases.

# Contents

Hannibal
(St. Petersburg)

Illinois

Missouri
Territory

Missouri

Missouri River

St. Louis

Cairo

Ohio River

Steamboat
wreck

Kentucky

Compromise
(Grangerford house)

White River

Tennessee

Arkansas River

Indian
Territory

Arkansas

Memphis

Mississippi River

Greenville
(Wilks house)

Republic
of
Texas

Red River

Mississippi

Louisiana

N
W   E
S

MISSISSIPPI RIVER
VALLEY, ABOUT 1840

Baton Rouge

New Orleans

☐ Slave area
■ Free area

## Chapter 1
# A Band of Robbers

You don't know me unless you've read *The Adventures of Tom Sawyer.* That's a book written by Mr. Mark Twain. In it he told the truth. Of course, he stretched a few things. But almost everybody lies sometimes.

At the end of that book, Tom and I found a lot of money hidden in a cave. It made us rich. We got six thousand dollars each—all gold.

"Huckleberry! Come inside right now!"

That's the widow Douglas. She took me in after my pap disappeared. As I was saying, Tom and I found a heap of gold. Then Judge Thatcher put it in the bank for us so that we'd earn interest. Now we get a dollar a day each. That's more money than I know what to do with.

"Huckleberry! Your supper is getting cold!"

The widow Douglas was trying to "civilize" me. I didn't like being civilized. For one thing, I had to wear new clothes. They made me feel all sweaty and cramped. And I had to study spelling with Miss Watson, the widow's sister.

When I couldn't stand it anymore, I ran away. I got into my old rags and took off for the woods. But Tom Sawyer came after me. He wanted to start a band of robbers. He said I could join if I went back to the widow's house and acted respectable. So I went back.

"You poor lost lamb," the widow cried when I walked in the door. She put me in

new clothes again, just like before. And she gave me supper at the same time each evening. I didn't much care for the widow's cooking. I like my food all slopped together so that the juices mix around.

After supper I'd sit in my room by the window, and try to think about something cheerful. It was no use. I felt awful lonely.

One night, the stars were shining. Far out in the woods I could hear a ghost moan. It made me scared. Then a spider crawled up my shoulder. I flipped it off. It landed in the candle, curled up, and died. Everybody knows that's bad luck. So I got even more scared.

After a while, the town clock went clang, clang, clang, twelve times. It was midnight. A minute later I heard a rustle in the trees, and a low voice.

"Me-yow! Me-yow!"

That was no cat. It was Tom Sawyer. I climbed out of the window and onto the shed. Sure enough, when I reached the clump of trees near the garden, Tom was waiting for me.

"Where we goin'?" I whispered.

"To the cave."

We tiptoed around the edge of the garden, through the trees. When we passed by the kitchen, I tripped over a root and fell. My body made a big thump.

Tom lay down beside me and we tried to keep still. The light was on in the kitchen. We could see Miss Watson's slave, Jim, sitting in the doorway.

"Who's that?" he said. He came out and stood a few feet away from us. Luckily, he didn't see us. My face itched bad. Then my arm itched, and the back of my neck. Doesn't that always seem to happen just when you really *have* to keep still? But I didn't move.

After a while, Jim went inside. Tom and I continued out through the woods. Joe Harper, Ben Rogers, and two or three other boys were waiting for us at the top of Sumner's Hill.

We could see the village lights below. At the bottom of the hill we found a row-boat and unhitched it. We went down the river until we got to a big scar in the hillside. That's where the cave was. It was dark and sweaty. Tom lit a candle.

"We'll start a band of robbers and call it Tom Sawyer's Gang," Tom said. "If you want to join, you have to write your name in blood."

The smaller boys began to cry.

"If anyone tells our secrets," Tom said,

"we'll kill his family."

"But Huck doesn't have a family," Ben said. "What about him?"

"He's got a father," Tom shot back.

"But nobody knows where he is."

They talked it over. None of the boys knew what to do. I was about to cry. Then I offered them Miss Watson to kill.

Everybody said: "Okay. She'll do. You can be in the group, Huck." Then we all stuck a pin in our fingers and signed our names in blood.

## Chapter 2
## Pap Returns

The next morning, Miss Watson scrubbed the grease off my clothes without saying a word. I could tell that I'd disappointed her, so I tried to behave for a while. I didn't want her to think that I'd grow up to be like Pap.

He hadn't been seen in more than a year. I didn't care. He always tried to beat me. People said that a body had been found in the river up north. It was the same size as Pap's, and had the same long, scraggly hair. But then I heard that the body had been floating on its back. I knew very well that a drowned man floats on his face, not his back. So I figured it wasn't Pap, but a woman dressed up in a man's clothes. I knew Pap would return.

Three or four months went by. I tried to stay out of trouble. I went to school most of the time, and could pretty much spell, read, and write. Living in a house and sleeping in a bed weren't much fun. Before the cold weather came I'd slide down the roof and sleep in the woods. Every once in a while, I'd sneak out with Tom and the other boys.

I liked the old ways, but the new ways weren't too bad. The widow said I was coming along. She put in a good word for me with Miss Watson, even when I messed up.

One morning at breakfast, I spilled salt all over the table. I grabbed some and threw it over my left shoulder—to keep away bad luck.

"Huckleberry!" Miss Watson yelled. "You're making a mess!"

"There, there," the widow said. "Let him be."

But that wasn't going to keep away the bad luck. After breakfast, I got all worried and shaky. I moped around, then climbed over the fence near the garden. An inch of snow had fallen in the night.

Somebody's tracks were in the snow. They looked like boot prints, about the

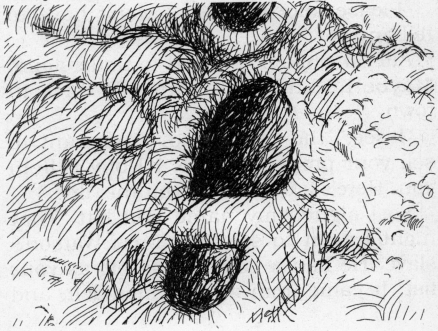

size of Pap's. So I ran as fast as I could to Judge Thatcher's.

"You're all out of breath," the judge said. "Did you come for your interest?"

"No, sir," I said. "I don't want any of it."

That confused him some, so he offered it to me again.

"No, sir," I said again. "I don't want my interest or *any* of the six thousand. I want you to take it—all of it!"

He looked surprised. "What do you mean, my boy?"

"Please take it! Then I won't have to tell any lies."

After a while he seemed to understand. Maybe he knew that Pap was back in town.

"I see," the judge said. "You want to sell your property to me. I'll buy it from you. Here's a dollar. Sign on this line."

So I signed my name and left. That night I went to see Jim, Miss Watson's slave. He had a hair ball as big as your fist. It came from an ox's stomach, and

Jim used it to do magic. I told him that I'd seen Pap's tracks in the snow.

"What's he going to do?" I asked Jim. "Is he going to stay?"

Jim held the hair ball up to his ear. He shook it some, then listened some more. "It won't talk without money," he said.

I didn't mention the dollar the judge had given me. Instead, I pulled a counterfeit quarter out of my pocket. Jim smelled it and bit it and rubbed it.

"This'll do," he said. He put the quarter under the hair ball. Then he leaned down and listened. "It'll tell your whole fortune if you want."

"Go on," I said.

So the hair ball talked to Jim and Jim told me what it said: "Your pap isn't sure yet what he is going to do. But you're all right. You're going to have a lot of trouble in your life, and a lot of joy."

That night, when I lit my candle and went up to my room, there sat Pap.

## Chapter 3
# Into the Woods

**P**ap was almost fifty, and he looked it. His hair was all tangled and greasy. It hung down over his face. Still, you could see his eyes shining through, as if he were behind vines. His hair was black, just like his whiskers. His face, what you could see of it, was fish-belly white.

"They say you can read and write now," Pap said. "You think you're better than your father, don't you?"

"Maybe I do, maybe I don't," I said. I

wasn't as afraid of Pap as I used to be.

"Who said you could meddle with such highfalutin business?"

"The widow."

"Well, I'll teach her," Pap said. "You're my son, and I'll raise you to be just as ignorant as I am!" He picked up a book and asked me to read from it.

"General Washington was a great leader . . ."

"So, they didn't lie! You *can* read! Well, smarty pants, if I ever catch you putting on airs again I'll whip you good."

He mumbled something I couldn't hear. Then he said: "They tell me you're rich."

"They lie."

"Don't give me any sass. Get me that money tomorrow—or else."

"I don't have any money, I told you."

"Then Judge Thatcher has it," Pap said. "Get it from him." He asked me how much money I had in my pocket.

"Only a dollar," I said.

"Hand it over! Now!"

He took it and bit it to see if it was good. Then he left to buy some whiskey. When he climbed out the window, he fell off the roof and broke his arm.

Over the next few months, Pap got into plenty of trouble. He tried to get the money from Judge Thatcher, but the judge wouldn't give it to him. The judge and the widow went to court to see if they could take me away from Pap. But the law is a slow business.

Pap whipped me a few times for going to school. I went anyway. Not that I wanted to. But I figured I'd go just to spite him.

Pretty soon spring came. The widow yelled at Pap for hanging around all the time. So one day he snatched me on the way home from school, and dragged me down to the river.

We rowed for about three miles, stopping on the Illinois shore. Illinois is on the other side of the river from St. Petersburg, Missouri, where the widow lives.

There were a lot of trees on the shore, but no houses. Finally, we found a log hut deep in the woods. Pap kept me with him all the time, so I couldn't run away.

He had a gun, which I think he had stolen. We fished and hunted, and ate whatever we caught. Every once in a while he would lock me in and go down to the general store. He'd trade fish and game for whiskey, get drunk, and come home and beat me.

After about two months, my clothes got

to be all rags and dirt, just the way I like them. I didn't know how I'd ever get used to life at the widow's again. There you had to wash every day, and eat on a plate.

But I grew sick of Pap hitting me all the time. So one morning, after he'd locked me in the cabin, I decided to escape. There was a rusty saw stuck between the roof and the top of a wall. I greased it up and cut a hole through one of the walls. I wasn't sure when Pap would be home, so I had to work fast.

After the hole was cut, I carried a sack of corn meal, two blankets, and a tin cup down to the river. Then I took Pap's gun and went up into the woods to hunt for birds. Instead I saw a wild pig. I shot it and took it back to the cabin. When I cut open its throat, blood splashed all over the floor.

I dragged the pig down to the river, leaving a trail of blood behind me. Then I dumped the pig in the water. That way,

Pap would think I'd been murdered. They'd look for the murderers, and maybe look in the river for my dead body, but they wouldn't look farther for me. I wished Tom Sawyer could see me. He always likes a good adventure.

Just before dark, I searched for a canoe I'd seen under a tree. I dropped it into the river, loaded it with my supplies, and waited for the moon to rise. I decided to sail down to Jackson's Island and hide there, since I knew it pretty well.

The current was swift that night, so it didn't take me long to get there. By dawn I could see a ferry boat out on the river. It was full of people. I knew they were looking for me.

# Chapter 4
# The Search Party

The ferry boat drifted in so close that I could see everybody on it. There was Pap, Judge Thatcher, Joe Harper, and Tom Sawyer. Even Tom's old Aunt Polly was on board.

Everybody talked about the murder. Then the captain broke in and said: "Look sharp! Maybe he's washed ashore."

They crowded together and leaned over the rails, practically in my face. I could

see them, but they couldn't see me.

"Stand away!" the captain yelled. He fired a cannon across the river. The reason you fire a cannon is to get dead bodies to rise to the surface.

Joe Harper shouted that he saw something. So everybody huddled together again. But all he had seen was a broken branch floating down the river.

I was getting hungry, but I had to wait for them to leave. Pretty soon, they

sailed off. I knew they wouldn't come after me again.

Once they were gone, I made a kind of tent with my blankets. That way I could put things under it whenever it rained. Toward sundown, I caught a catfish and hacked it open with my saw. Then I made a fire and ate supper. Before going to sleep, I just sat by the edge of the river, counting the stars. It was a satisfying feeling.

Next day I explored around the island. There were plenty of strawberries and green grapes to feast on. I had my gun along, but it was just for protection.

I saw a neat place at the top of a hill, but I wanted to get back before sundown. About a mile away from camp, near a clump of bushes, I almost stepped on a snake. I took off as fast as I could. All of a sudden I came upon the ashes of a campfire that was still smoking. My heart jumped into my lungs.

I snuck back on tiptoes. Then I heard a rustle in the leaves. So I climbed into a tree and stayed real quiet. I was glad I had my gun with me.

When the sun went down, it got kind of cold. But I was afraid to move. I was getting hungry, too. So I munched on the strawberries in my pocket.

I must've dozed off for a few hours. When I awoke, the sky was light gray. There on the ground lay a man with a blanket over his head. He was about six feet tall. Pretty soon he stretched his arms and threw off the blanket.

It was Miss Watson's Jim!

"Hello, Jim!" I called, jumping out of the tree.

He bounced up and stared at me with a frightened look in his eyes.

"Go and get in the river where you belong, ghost!" he said. "And please don't do nothing to ol' Jim. I was always your friend."

It didn't take me long to explain that I

wasn't dead. Boy, was I glad to see Jim. Now I wouldn't be lonely.

"Let's make a fire and get some breakfast," I said.

"What's the use of making a fire if all we have are strawberries?" Jim said.

"Is that all you've eaten since you got here, Jim?"

"I couldn't get anything else," Jim said. "I don't have a gun."

"How long've you been on the island?"

"I came here the night after you was killed."

"I told you, Jim, I ain't dead." Then I explained how I'd hacked up the pig in the cabin.

"You sure is smart," Jim said. "Tom Sawyer couldn't've done better."

That day we caught three or four catfish. After supper, we lay on the grass, relaxing. I asked Jim why he'd come to the island.

"Maybe I'd better not tell you," he said.

"Why not, Jim?"

"You won't tell on me, will you?"

"Of course not!"

"Well, I run off," Jim said.

"Jim!"

"Now, Huck, you said you wouldn't tell."

"I promise I won't. I'm not going back anyway. But why did you do it, Jim?"

"I heard ol' Miss Watson say that she was going to sell me—to somebody in New Orleans. She treats me pretty rough, but a new master could be a whole lot worse!"

"Why would she sell you?"

"She didn't want to. But I heard her tell the widow that she could get eight hundred dollars for me. I guess she needed the money."

"Well, now it's just you and me, Jim. We don't have much, but we'll get by."

"I feel like a rich man," Jim said. "I have you as a friend, and I own myself— and I'm worth eight hundred dollars!"

## Chapter 5
# A Floating House

In the morning, I took Jim to that place I'd seen the day before. First we had to climb a steep hill covered with thick bushes. We tramped all over the place, until we came to a cavern.

It was the size of two or three rooms bunched together. Jim wanted to move our stuff in right away, and set up camp.

"Nah," I said. "We don't want to have to be climbing up and down the hill all the time."

"We'll be safer in here," Jim said. "If anybody comes to the island, they'll never find us. Besides, I think it's going to rain."

So we went back and hid the canoe. Then we lugged our supplies up the hill. At the edge of the cavern, the floor stuck out a bit. It was a good place to build a fire. So we built it there, and cooked up some dinner.

We spread the blankets inside for a carpet, and laid our supplies against the wall. Pretty soon the sky darkened. Every now and then you'd hear thunder let go with an awful crash. Rain began to fall in a fury.

"Jim, this is nice," I said. "I wouldn't want to be anywhere else but here."

"Well, you wouldn't be here," Jim said, "if it hadn't been for me. You'd have been down in the woods without any dinner. Getting drowned, too. You couldn't see it was about to rain."

Well, I knew he was right about that. I

just sat back, nibbling on a hunk of fish and some hot corn bread.

For the next few days, the river kept rising on the island. The water was three or four feet deep in the low places, so we could paddle all over in the canoe. But we tried not to move around during the day too much. We didn't want anybody to see us.

One night, we found a piece of a raft, about twelve feet wide and fifteen feet long. Another night, we saw a frame

house coming down the river. It was two stories high, and kind of tilted over. We paddled out and got aboard, climbing in at an upstairs window.

It was still dark out, so we tied our canoe to the house and waited for a while. When daylight came, we saw that the floating house had stopped near the foot of the island. We could make out a table and two old chairs, and some clothes hanging against the wall. Then Jim saw something lying on the floor in

the far corner. It looked like a man.

"Hello!" Jim said. But it didn't budge.

Then I hollered: "Hello! Hello!"

"That man ain't asleep," Jim said. "He's dead." He went and bent down and looked. "Yep," Jim said. "He's dead all right. Been shot in the back. Come on, Huck, move along. Don't look at his face. It's too awful."

Jim threw some old rags over him. Then we grabbed whatever we could—a tin lantern, a butcher's knife, some can-

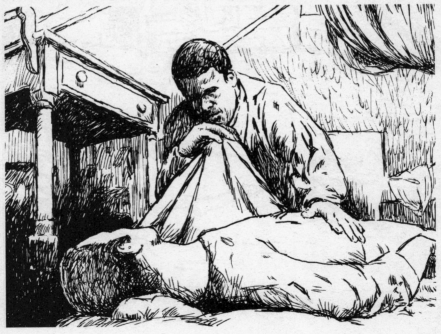

dles, two dresses, a sunbonnet, and a bed quilt. We even found eight dollars in silver sewed into the lining of an old coat.

"Remember the other day," I said, "when I found the snakeskin at the top of the ridge?"

"I surely do," Jim said.

"You said it was bad luck to touch a snakeskin. Here's your bad luck! We found all of this stuff, and eight dollars besides."

"Never you mind," Jim said. "That bad luck's a' comin'."

"Sometimes I just don't understand you," I said.

When we were ready to shove off, I had Jim lie down in the canoe. I covered him up real good with the quilt, in case someone happened by. If anybody saw him, they'd know he was a runaway slave and try to catch him.

The canoe was full, so we drifted slowly back to the island. Luckily, we got home safe.

## Chapter 6
# Dressing Up

**A**fter breakfast, I wanted to talk about the dead man.

"A man who ain't buried is more likely to cause trouble," Jim said, "than a man who is planted and comfortable."

That sounded reasonable, so I didn't say any more. But I still wanted to know who'd shot the man, and why. It made me think about my own murder. I wondered what everybody in the village thought about it.

One day I decided to slip across the river, to see if I could find out anything. Jim liked the idea. But he said I should go after dark. It would be safer that way. Then he looked at the clothes we'd found in the floating house.

"You could put on one of those dresses we found," he said, "and pretend that you're a girl."

I put on the calico dress. Jim said that it was a pretty good fit. He helped me turn up my trouser legs to the knees.

Then I put on the sunbonnet and tied it under my chin.

"I don't think anybody'll recognize you now," Jim said.

All day I practiced walking like a girl, just to get the hang of it. Jim said to quit pulling up my dress to get at my pants pocket. It was tough being a girl.

After dark, I went up the river in the canoe. The drift of the current left me at the bottom of the village, below where the ferry stops. I tied up and started along the bank.

There was a light burning in a shack that had been empty for a long time. I peeked in at the window and saw a woman sitting by a candle, knitting. I didn't know her face. That was lucky, because I knew almost everybody in the village. I decided to knock at the door.

"Come in," the woman said, and I did. She looked at me with her little gray eyes. "What's your name?" she asked.

"Sarah Williams," I replied.

"Do you live in this neighborhood?"

"No, ma'am. I come from a town about seven miles away. I walked here."

"I bet you're hungry," she said.

"Not really. I stopped at a farm along the way, and had somethin' to eat. That's what makes me so late."

"Why did you come all this way?"

"My mama's sick," I said, "and out of money. I came to tell my uncle."

"What's his name?"

"Abner Moore. Do you know him?"

"No, but I don't know everybody yet. I've only lived here two weeks." Then she said: "You'd better spend the night here, since it's so late."

"No, thank you, ma'am," I said. "I'll just rest for a while, then be on my way."

She didn't want me to go by myself, because of the dark. "My husband will be home soon," she said. "He can walk you to your uncle's." Then she started talking about the town, and about how I'd been murdered.

"Who did it?" I asked.

"Some think old Finn killed his son."

"Really?" I said, trying to act surprised.

"Most everybody thought that at first. Then they decided that the boy was killed by a runaway slave named Jim."

"Jim?" I cried. I decided that I'd better keep quiet. I didn't want to give anything away. Turns out, she'd hardly noticed me. She kept right on talking.

"That slave ran off the same night

Huck Finn was killed. There's a reward for him—three hundred dollars."

"Really?"

"And there's a reward for old Finn. Two hundred dollars."

"That's quite a bit of money," I said.

"He came to town the morning after the murder and told about it. He even went searching with everybody on the ferry boat. But right afterward, he up and disappeared."

She put her ball of yarn on the table. "A few days later, he came back and started boo-hooing to Judge Thatcher about the boy's money. Now folks think that old Finn murdered Huck, just to get the boy's six thousand dollars."

"Has everybody quit thinking that Jim did it?" I asked.

"Not everybody. A lot of people think he's guilty. They'll find him soon. Then they can force him to confess."

"Are they after him?"

"Of course they are. Three hundred

dollars doesn't come along every day! Some folks think Jim isn't far from here."

"Why do they think that?" I said. I was getting awful nervous. I picked up her ball of yarn but dropped it. So I had to rewind it, hoping I was doing it right.

"The couple next door said that nobody ever goes to Jackson's Island," the woman said. "But I'm sure that I saw smoke over there the other day. The slave's probably hiding there."

"Maybe it was the fog?" I said.

"Maybe," she said. "But I'm gonna send my husband over to that island when he gets back." I was shaking like a leaf.

"What did you say your name was, little girl?" she said.

"M—Mary Williams, ma'am."

"I thought you said it was Sarah."

"Yes, ma'am, I did. It's Sarah Mary Williams." I wished I was out of there.

"What's your real name?" she demanded. "Is it Bill, or Tom, or Bob?"

I didn't know what to do. "Please don't

poke fun at a poor girl like me, ma'am."

"Well, no girl or woman ever rolls yarn the way you did. You were trying too hard—and *still* doing it wrong!"

I had to think fast. "Well, ma'am, my mother and father are dead," I began, "and the law has bound me to a mean ol' farmer. So I ran away. I've come to see my uncle, here in Goshen."

"Child, this ain't Goshen!" the woman said. "This is St. Petersburg. Goshen is ten miles up the river."

"Oh, my!" I said. "Well, then, I'd really better be going. I want to reach Goshen before daybreak." I tore out of there as fast as I could. As I got to the canoe, the clock began to strike. One—two—

It was eleven o'clock! There was no time to waste.

## Chapter 7
# The Shipwreck

**W**hen I reached the island, I started a fire where my old camp used to be. Then I ran through the trees and up the ridge to the cavern. Jim was sound asleep.

"Get up, Jim!" I shouted. "We have to hurry. They're after us!"

Jim didn't ask any questions. But the way he worked showed how scared he was. We loaded everything onto the raft, then put out the campfire at the cavern.

I got into the canoe and paddled out into the water, to see if anybody was coming. Not a boat in sight. But stars and shadows aren't good to see by.

We tied the canoe to the back of the raft, then glided slowly down the river. We made a plan: If a boat came along, we'd ditch the raft and take off in the canoe, go over to the Illinois shore. It was lucky that a boat didn't come, because we'd loaded everything we had onto the raft, including the gun.

When day broke, we tied up on a sandbar. Jim hacked off some tree branches. He covered the raft with them, to disguise it. We lay there all day, watching the steamboats spin down the river. I told Jim about the woman in St. Petersburg, how she'd figured me out. He said she sounded real smart.

After sunset, we poked our heads out of the tree branches. Jim looked up the river and I looked down. Nothing in sight. With some wooden planks, he built a tipi

on the raft. That way, we'd be protected against the rain. He even made a place to build a fire in cold or sloppy weather, and an extra oar in case one broke.

The next night, we sailed down the river. We caught fish, talked, and took a swim now and then to keep off sleepiness. It was fun drifting beneath the stars. We passed small towns, some of them up on dark hillsides. Nothing happened to us that night, or the next, or the next.

The fifth night, we passed St. Louis. It was all lit up. I'd heard that twenty or thirty thousand people lived there! Seeing that wonderful spread of lights at two in the morning, I finally believed it.

Every night I'd slip ashore somewhere, to buy ten cents' worth of meal or bacon. Sometimes I'd borrow a chicken that was wandering around. Mornings, I'd slip into farmers' fields and get a watermelon, a pumpkin, or some new corn. We lived pretty well.

Below St. Louis one night, there was a big storm. So we stayed in the fort. Rain poured down in a solid sheet. After a while I called out to Jim: "Looky there!"

A steamboat had crashed against a rock, and we were drifting straight toward it.

"Let's go aboard!" I said.

Jim was against the idea. "What if somebody's standing guard?"

"Who would risk his life on a night like this?" I said. "That boat's likely to break apart any minute."

"Exactly," Jim said.

"Tom Sawyer would never pass up an adventure like this."

Jim grumbled some, but finally agreed.

The current jerked us forward. We almost hit the ship. We tied up the raft, then snuck up onto the deck. At the door of the captain's cabin, we heard voices! Jim said he felt sick.

"Never mind," I said. "We'll go back to the raft."

Just then a voice cried out, "Please don't! I swear I won't tell!"

Another voice, pretty loud, said, "That's a lie! You always want more than your share." By this time, Jim had headed for the raft. I thought to myself: Tom Sawyer wouldn't back out now. So I didn't.

I got on my hands and knees and crept into the captain's cabin. It was dark, but I could see a man stretched out on the floor. His hands and feet were tied up. Two men stood over him. One of them had a lantern in his hand. The other had a gun.

"Please don't!" the man on the floor said.

"I ought to," the guy with the gun said. "You're a mean skunk."

Then the two guys turned toward the door. I crawled backwards as fast as I could. It was dark, so they didn't see me.

"Let's kill him," said the guy with the gun.

"We don't need to," the second guy

said. "In about two hours, this wreck'll break apart. Let's load our boat with the loot, and shove for shore." I headed for the deck, sorry I'd come aboard in the first place.

"Jim," I whispered. "There's a gang of murderers up here. If we don't find their boat and cut it loose, one of them's going to be in a bad fix."

Jim climbed back onto the deck.

"But if we find their boat," I went on. "we can put *all* of 'em in a bad fix. Then the sheriff will find them."

"Oh, no!" Jim cried. "The raft just broke loose! And here we are!"

## Chapter 8
# Trapped!

**W**e were trapped! My legs almost collapsed beneath me. We *had* to find the murderers' boat now.

I looked out across the dark water. No sign of it. The rain had stopped, but the wind still blew hard. Jim said he was so scared he could hardly move.

"Come on, Jim," I said. "If we get stuck on this wreck, we'll *really* be in a fix." We groped our way toward the back of the ship.

"Look!" Jim whispered. "There she is." Sure enough, there was the rowboat. It shook mightily in the choppy waters.

Another second and I would have been on board. But just then the cabin door opened. One of the men stuck his head out. I thought I was a goner.

"Hide that lantern, Bill!" he yelled. He flung a bag into the rowboat and got in himself. Then Bill came out.

"Shove off!"

I could hardly stand up I was so weak.

But Bill said: "Wait, Packard. Did you search him?"

"Didn't you?" Packard said.

"No. So he still has the cash on him."

"Let's go back," Packard said. "No sense in leaving money behind." They got out and went inside. The door slammed behind them.

I hopped into the boat. Jim tumbled in after me. I pulled out my knife and cut the rope. Away we went!

We drifted down the river fast. In a few

seconds, we were a hundred yards below the wreck. Jim grabbed the oars, and we headed for our raft.

Then I began to worry about the men. It was awful, even for murderers, to be in such a fix. I said to Jim: "The first light we see, I'll go ashore. You can hide in the boat while I look for somebody to rescue the gang."

Just then, it began to storm again. The rain poured down, and we never saw a light. Soon there was a black thing floating a little way ahead of us.

It was the raft—with the canoe still fastened to the back! We were mighty glad to find it. We could see a light now, way down to the right, on shore. I said that I would go into the village to look for somebody.

As Jim climbed onto the raft, I handed the murderers' loot down to him. "Float down a little further," I told him. "When you've gone about two miles, shine a

light and keep it burning till I get there."

I took the rowboat and headed for the village. Soon I could see a lantern hanging from the ferry deck. I rowed over and went to look for the watchman. He was asleep on the other side of the deck, his head between his knees. I climbed up and gave his shoulder a few shoves. I began to cry.

He sat up, startled. "Don't cry, bub," he said. "What's wrong?"

"Pap and mam and sis—"

"What's the matter with 'em?"

"They're in an awful lot of trouble."

"Where are they?" he said, leaning forward in his chair.

"On the wreck."

"What are they doin' there?"

I made up a yarn about how they were on board with a Miss Hooker. I said her uncle was Jim Hornback, one of the richest men in the South.

"Could you go and rescue them?" I asked.

"I'd like to. But who will pay for it?"

"Well, Miss Hooker told me that Old Hornback—"

"Okay, son. You head for the village. Have the folks take you to Jim Hornback's place. Tell him I'll have his niece safe in no time, if he'll foot the bill."

I pretended to head for the village. As soon as he turned around, I went back to the rowboat. I sat quietly for a moment. It made me happy that I'd saved the murderers' lives. I wished the widow could have seen me. She'd have been proud.

But before long, the wreck floated by. A cold shiver went through me. I saw in a minute that no one could have survived. "Hello!" I called. No answer.

Then the ferry came along. The watchman sniffed around for Miss Hooker's remains. After a while he gave up and went ashore. I sped down the river.

It was a long time before Jim's light appeared. When it did, it seemed to be a thousand miles away. By the time I got there, the sun was rising. We headed for an island, hid the raft, and sank the murderers' rowboat. Then we slept like dead men.

# Chapter 9
# Polly-voo-franzy?

**W**hen we woke up, we inspected the murderers' loot. There were blankets, clothes, and a lot of books. Neither one of us had ever been that rich.

We lay around in the woods all afternoon, just talking. I told Jim what had happened to the wreck.

"These kinds of things are adventures," I said.

"I don't want no more adventures," Jim said. Then he told me something I

hadn't thought about. "When we lost the raft," he said, "I figured I was a goner either way. Either I was gonna drown, or be saved. And if someone had saved me, they'd have sent me back to get the reward for catching a runaway slave."

Jim was right. If he'd been turned in, Miss Watson would've sold him for sure. Jim was always right. For a slave, he had a lot of smarts.

I took out one of the books and read to

him about kings and dukes. "They dress up in fancy clothes," I said, "and call each other 'Your Majesty' and 'Your Lordship,' instead of 'mister.'"

I could tell Jim was mighty interested. "I didn't know there were so many of 'em," he said. "Unless you count the kings in a deck of cards."

I told him about Louis XVI, and how he got his head chopped off in France a long time ago. "He had a little boy, the Dolphin, who would have been king," I

said. "But they locked him up in jail. Some say he died there."

"Poor little chap."

"Others think he got away and came to America."

"That's good," Jim said. "But he'd be lonely here. We don't have no kings."

Somehow, we got into a long conversation about why French people speak French. "If someone were to say *polly-voo-franzy*," I explained, "they would just be saying, 'Do you speak French?' "

"Well, it's wrong," Jim said. "It don't make no sense."

I tried to show him that it *did* make sense. "Listen, Jim. Does a cat talk like we do?"

"No."

"Does a cow?"

"A cow don't, neither."

"It's natural and right for them to talk different from each other," I said. "Ain't it?"

"Of course."

"And it's natural for them to talk

different from *us*, right?" I asked him.

"Surely."

"So why ain't it natural for a *Frenchman* to talk different from us? Answer me that."

"Come on, Huck. Is a cat a man?"

"No."

"Then there ain't no sense in a cat talkin' like a man. Is a cow a man?"

"No," I said.

"Well then, a cow has no business talking like a man," Jim said. "Neither does a cat. But is a Frenchman a man?"

"Yes, of course."

"Then why don't he talk like a man?"

I saw it was no use wasting words. Jim just didn't get it. So I quit arguin'.

## Chapter 10
## No More Tricks

**W**e figured that it would take us three nights to get down to Cairo, Illinois. That's where the Mississippi meets the Ohio River. There we'd sell the raft and board a steamboat going north, up the Ohio. We wanted to go to the free states, where slavery wasn't allowed. Then we'd be out of trouble.

The second night, a fog rolled in. We steered toward a sandbar, hoping to tie the raft to a tree. But when I paddled ahead in the canoe, all I could find were little saplings. I tied the raft line around one of them.

There was a stiff current. The raft came booming down so fast, it tore the tiny tree out by its roots. The raft darted away, with Jim on it. I took off after it in the canoe, smack into a solid white fog. You couldn't see ten yards ahead.

From far away, I heard a small whoop. My spirits rose. Then, for a long time, I heard nothing. I'd lost Jim! It can be

mighty lonesome in a fog when you're by yourself. If you don't believe me, try it.

For the next hour I heard whoops now and then. But I kept running up against sandbars. Finally, I got back into the open river. No sign of a whoop anywhere. I was so tired I lay down in the canoe for a catnap.

I must've slept for a long time. When I awoke, the stars were shining and the fog was gone. The canoe was drifting slowly down a big bend in the river. At first I didn't know where I was. The river seemed huge, with thick trees on either side of it.

I saw a black speck downstream and took off after it. But it was just a couple of logs fastened together. Then I chased after another speck. This time it was the raft.

When I reached Jim, he was asleep. His right arm hung over the steering oar. The other oar was smashed in two. Leaves, twigs, and dirt covered Jim's legs.

I tied up the canoe, then crept aboard

the raft. I lay down under Jim's nose and stretched my fists against him.

"Have I been asleep, Jim?" I said, yawning. "Why didn't you wake me?"

"Is that you, Huck? Where were you?"

"What's the matter with you, Jim?"

"I thought you'd drowned!"

"You must've been dreaming. I've been here all along."

"Huck Finn, you look me in the eyes. Haven't you been up the river?"

"I haven't been anywhere. Where would I go?"

"Didn't that raft line pull loose in the fog?" Jim said. He looked awful upset, but I was having fun.

"What fog, Jim?"

"Didn't I whoop until I hit up against some islands and almost drown?"

"Well, this is too much for me, Jim. We've been sitting here all night, talking. You just went to sleep about ten minutes ago. You must've been dreaming."

"How could I dream so much in ten

minutes, Huck?" Jim wanted to know.

"I don't know, but none of that stuff happened."

"Then I guess I did dream it. But it was the most powerful dream I ever had." Then he started to tell me what the dream meant.

The whoops were warnings, Jim said. The sandbars represented trouble we'd get into with terrible people. But if we minded our own business, then we

would get out of the fog. We would get back onto the big, clear river, which represented the free states.

"That's all interpreted very well, Jim," I said. "But what do *these* things stand for?" I pointed to the leaves and rubbish on the raft, and the smashed oar.

Jim was furious. "What do they stand for?" he said. "I'll tell you what! My heart! It was broken when you were lost. And when I woke up and found you safe

and sound, tears came to my eyes. But all you could think about was how much of a fool you could make of ol' Jim."

He got up slowly and walked into the raft's tipi. I felt so mean. I'd never apologized to a slave before. That just wasn't done. But I finally went inside and told Jim that I was sorry.

After that I didn't play any more mean tricks on him. I wouldn't have done that one, either, if I'd known it would make him feel so bad.

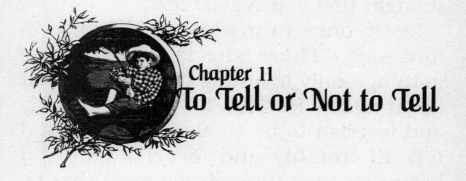

## Chapter 11
# To Tell or Not to Tell

That night, we set out behind a huge boat. The river was wide, the air hot and muggy. We talked about Cairo, and wondered whether we would know it when we got to it.

I said that we probably wouldn't. I had heard that there were only about a dozen houses in Cairo. If they weren't lit up, how would we know we were passing a town? Jim said that if the two big rivers joined there, we'd be able to tell.

"We'd better ask directions," I said. "Just in case." I decided to paddle ashore at the first town that showed a light. Jim thought that was a good idea.

Every once in a while he'd jump up and say: "There she is!" But it was nothing—only lightning bugs. So he'd sit down again. He said he felt all trembly and feverish to be so close to freedom. I felt all trembly and feverish, too. I'd begun to get it through my head that he *was* almost free. And who was to blame? Me! I was going against everything folks had ever taught me.

I could have paddled ashore and told somebody that he was running for his freedom. But I didn't. My conscience asked me: "What did poor Miss Watson ever do to you? And now you're going to let her slave go free, without saying a word to stop him."

I got to feeling so bad and low that I almost wished I were dead. I fidgeted up and down the raft, hating myself. Jim

fidgeted up and down past me. Neither one of us could keep still. Every time he danced around and said, "There's Cairo," I thought that if it *was* Cairo, I'd die.

He talked out loud all the time, while I was talking to myself. The first thing he'd do when he got to a free state, he said, was earn some money. When he'd saved enough, he would buy back his wife. She was a slave on a farm near St. Petersburg. Then they would both work to buy their two children.

Here was a slave, who I was helping to run away, saying out loud that he would steal his children. Children belonging to a man I didn't even know, who'd never done me any harm.

I was sorry to hear Jim talk that way. I was so confused! My conscience stirred me even more. Finally, I told it: "Let up on me! I'll paddle ashore at the first light and tell." I felt much better after that.

Soon I saw a light on the shore. Jim sang out, "We're safe, Huck! Good ol'

Cairo is here at last!" He sure was happy.

"I'll take the canoe," I said, "and go check. It might not be, you know."

He got the canoe ready and gave me the paddle. As I shoved off, he said: "Pretty soon I'll be shoutin' for joy. And I'll say, 'It's all thanks to Huck that I'm a free man.' "

## Chapter 12
# Missing Cairo

Jim didn't know that I was about to tell on him. He said, "I won't ever forget you, Huck. You're the best friend I've ever had—and the *only* friend I've got now."

After he said that, I didn't know what to do. I paddled a little slower, so I could think. When I was fifty yards away, Jim called out: "There you go, Huck. The only white man who's ever kept his promise to ol' Jim."

I felt sick. But I just *had* to turn him

in. Just then, a skiff came along with two men in it. They both had guns. One of them said: "What's that over there?"

"A piece of a raft," I said.

"Is it yours?"

"Yes, sir."

"Any men on it?"

"Only one, sir."

"Well, five slaves ran off tonight. Is your man white or black?"

I tried to answer, but the words wouldn't come. Finally I said: "He's white."

"We'll go and see for ourselves, won't we, Parker?"

"Of course, Wilson."

"I wish you would," I said, "because my pap's there and he's sick. Maybe you could tow us ashore."

"We're in a hurry, son! But I suppose we can help you."

After we had gone a few yards, I said, "Pap will be mighty grateful. Everybody else goes away when I ask for help."

"That's odd," Parker said. "Say, son, what's wrong with your father?"

"It's—well, it ain't anything much." They stopped rowing.

"That's a lie," Wilson said. "What's the matter with your pap? Tell the truth, boy."

"I will, sir. But please don't leave us."

They backed away. "Your pap has smallpox!" they both shouted. I didn't say a word.

"We'd like to help you," Wilson said. "But we don't want to get sick!"

"Tell you what," Parker said. "Float

down the river about twenty miles. You'll come to a town on the left. Go ashore. But don't be a fool this time. Tell people that your pap has chills and a fever."

They backed away some more, so the wind wouldn't carry germs toward them.

"I reckon your father's poor," Parker said. "So I'll put a twenty-dollar gold piece on this board. You grab it when it floats by. I'm sorry to leave you, but smallpox is contagious—and deadly."

"Hold on, Parker," Wilson said. "Here's

a twenty to put on the board for me. Good-bye, son. Do as Mr. Parker told you, and you'll be all right."

"That's so," Parker added. "And if you see any runaway slaves, nab them. You can make some money that way."

"Good-bye, sir," I said. "I won't let no runaway slaves get by me if I can help it."

They went away, and I went back to the raft. I felt bad because I knew I'd done wrong. Then I thought for a minute. What if I *had* done right, and given up Jim? I wouldn't have felt any better.

I went into the tipi, but Jim wasn't there. I looked all around. "Jim!" I called.

"Here I am, Huck. They gone?" He was hiding in the river, with just his nose out. I told him they'd left, so he came aboard.

"I thought they might find me," Jim said. "But you sure fooled 'em. You saved my life, and I'm never going to forget it."

We talked about the money. Forty dollars! Jim said we could afford steamboat tickets now, and still have plenty left over.

"Twenty more miles isn't far to go," Jim said. "But I wish we were already there."

Toward daybreak we tied up. Jim hid the raft good. Then he fixed everything in bundles, and got ready to quit rafting.

That night, we'd seen the lights of the town Parker told us about. I went off in the canoe to ask about it. Soon I saw a man out on the river, fishing.

"Mister," I said, "is that town Cairo?"

"Cairo? No! What are you, a fool?"

"What town is it, mister?"

"If you want to know, go and find out," he said.

I paddled back to the raft. Jim was dreadful disappointed. "Never mind," I said. "Cairo will be the next town."

We tied up on a sandbar for the day. I began to suspect something. So did Jim.

"Maybe we passed Cairo in the fog

that night," I said.

"Let's not talk about it," Jim said. "Slaves have no luck. I always knew that snakeskin would do us in."

"I wish I'd never seen that snakeskin!" I told him.

There was no sense going ashore. And we couldn't manage to get the raft going upstream. Our only hope was to start back in the canoe, and take our chances.

We slept all day beneath some cottonwood trees. After dark we returned to the raft. The canoe was gone! Neither of us said a word. We knew we had no choice but to continue downstream in the raft. When we got the chance, we'd buy a canoe to row back in.

We shoved out after dark. The air was so thick you couldn't tell the shape of the river. It got to be very late. Then along came a steamboat.

It was headed straight for us. We lit our lantern, hoping that the captain would see the raft. The boat was big,

and coming fast. The captain yelled! He jingled the bells to stop the engine.

There was a whistle of steam as Jim went overboard on one side. I went over on the other, as the boat smashed straight through the raft.

I dove as far down as I could, to give the wheel plenty of room. I must've stayed underwater for two minutes. Then I bounced to the top. I blew water out of my nose and breathed a bit.

I called to Jim a dozen times. No answer. So I grabbed a plank from the raft and struck out for shore.

I got there safely, and climbed up onto the bank. A quarter of a mile down the road, I came across a big, old-fashioned log house. I was going to walk by, but a bunch of dogs howled and barked at me. I knew better than to move another inch.

## Chapter 13
# Meeting the Grangerfords

In about half a minute, somebody spoke out of a window. "Who's there?" a voice said.

"George Jackson, sir."

"What do you want?"

"I only wanted to walk past your house, but the dogs wouldn't let me."

"Why are you prowling around this time of night?"

"I wasn't, sir. I fell overboard off the steamboat."

"If you're telling the truth, nobody will hurt you. But don't move. Stay right where you are."

"Yes, sir."

"Is anybody with you?"

"No, sir. Nobody." I heard people stirring inside the house. Then a light went on.

"Ain't you got any sense, Betsy?" the man said. "Put the light on the floor." Then he spoke to me. "George Jackson, do you know the Shepherdsons?"

"No, sir. Never heard of 'em."

"Then step forward. But not too fast. Otherwise we'll shoot."

I put one foot in front of the other, slowly. My heart pounded in my chest. The dogs were quiet, but they followed close behind me. When I got to the front steps, I heard somebody unbolt the door. I pushed it forward a little.

"That's enough," a voice said. "Now put your head in."

I could see a candle on the floor, and several people standing in the hall. Three

large men had their guns pointed at me.

The oldest was gray and about sixty. The other two were thirty or more, and very handsome. A sweet, gray-haired lady stood behind them. Behind her were two young women I couldn't see well. Betsy, the slave, stood on the other side of the room.

"I reckon it's all right," the old man said. "Come in."

As soon as I was in, he locked the door. He told the young men to follow him.

They went into a big parlor and stood in a corner, away from the windows.

Then they held the candle up and took a good look at me. "He ain't a Shepherdson," one of them said. The old man said he hoped I wouldn't mind being searched for guns. It was only a precaution.

"Make yourself at home," he said, after he saw that I didn't have any guns. "And tell us all about yourself."

"The poor thing is soaking wet," the old woman said, "and he's probably hungry."

"You're right, Rachel," the man said. "I forgot."

The old lady told one of her daughters to wake Buck. "Never mind, here he is," she said. "Buck, take this little stranger upstairs and get the wet clothes off of him. Give him some of yours."

Buck looked about my age—thirteen or fourteen. He didn't have anything on but a shirt. He dug one fist into his eyes. In the other he had a gun.

"Ain't no Shepherdsons around?" he asked.

"False alarm," they told him.

Buck and I went upstairs to his room. He gave me a shirt, some pants, and a short jacket to put on. Then he asked me my name, and told me about a young rabbit he'd caught in the woods.

"Say, how long you gonna stay here?" he asked. "I hope you stay forever. We could have a lot of fun."

He took me down to the kitchen. We ate cold corn bread, cold corn beef, butter, and buttermilk. It was the best food I'd come across yet. Everyone sat around talking while we ate.

They asked me a lot of questions. I told them stories about my pap and me living on a farm in the south of Arkansas. I said that I had a sister, Mary Ann, who had run off and got married.

"Bill went to find them and we didn't hear from him ever again," I said. "And Tom and Mort died. It was only Pap and

me left. After a while, he was just trimmed down to nothing, on account of his troubles."

They seemed interested, so I continued: "After Pap died, I left. I started up the river on the steamboat, and fell overboard. Right near the Kentucky-Tennessee border. That's how I came to be here."

They said I could stay as long as I wanted. Then everyone went to bed. I slept in Buck's room with him. But when I woke up, I forgot my new name. So I lay there for about an hour, trying to remember. When Buck woke up, I said: "Buck, can you spell?"

"Of course."

"Bet you can't spell my name."

"Yes, I can. G-o-r-g-e J-a-x-o-n."

"You did it!" I told him. "I didn't think you could. It's a tough name to spell without studying first." I sat down in private and tried to memorize the letters. I wanted to be ready if anyone asked me my name again.

## Chapter 14
## Miss Sophia's Letter

Buck's last name was Grangerford. His father, Colonel Grangerford, was an aristocrat—or "well-born," as the widow would say.

Every morning, he put on a clean shirt and a linen suit. The suit was so white it made your eyes hurt. Sundays he wore a blue military jacket with brass buttons. He owned more than a hundred slaves.

Each one of the Grangerford children had their own slave—even Buck. They gave me one, too. Since I wasn't used to having anybody wait on me, my slave had kind of a tough time.

There was another family nearby named Shepherdson. I'd see them riding on their horses. They were as rich as the Grangerfords.

One day Buck and I were out in the woods, hunting. As we crossed the road we heard a horse coming.

"Quick! Hide! Get behind those trees!" Buck said.

A young man came galloping down the road. He had a gun across his saddle. I'd seen him before. His name was Harney Shepherdson.

Just then, Buck's gun went off, and Harney's hat flew from his head. He raised his gun and rode straight toward our hiding place.

But we didn't wait. We ran through the woods until we got home. Colonel Grangerford seemed pleased when Buck told him what had happened. But

Buck's sister, Miss Sophia, turned pale. The color in her face didn't return until she knew the man wasn't hurt.

When I got Buck alone, down by the corn cribs, I said: "Did you want to kill that fellow?"

"You bet I did."

"What did he do to you?" I asked.

"Nothing."

"Then why did you want to kill him?"

"Because of the feud."

"What's a feud?" I said.

"Where were you raised? Don't you know what a feud is?"

"Never heard of it before. Tell me."

"A feud is this way," Buck said. "A man has a fight with another man and kills him. Then that other man's brother kills *him*. Then the other brothers, on both sides, go for one another. The cousins, too. Pretty soon everybody's dead, and there ain't no more feud." Buck scratched his head. "But it takes a long time."

"How long has this Grangerford—

Shepherdson feud been going on?"

"Thirty years. There was trouble about something, then a lawsuit. The man who lost the suit shot the man who won."

"What was the trouble about?"

"I don't know."

"Who done the shooting? Was it a Grangerford or a Shepherdson?"

"How do *I* know?" Buck said. "It was so long ago."

"Does anybody know?"

"Pa knows, I reckon, and maybe some of the older folks."

The next Sunday, we all went to church. The men took their guns along, and so did Buck. The sermon was about brotherly love. Later, they all agreed it was a good one.

About an hour after dinner, everybody took a nap. Buck and his dog were stretched out on the grass, sound asleep. I went upstairs to take a nap myself.

Miss Sophia followed me. She came into my room and shut the door.

"George, will you do me a favor?" she said softly.

"Sure."

"I left my Bible at church. Would you run and get it for me? But don't tell anybody where you're going."

So I slid out of the house and up the road. There was nobody at church, except maybe a hog or two. In summertime, they like a nice wood floor to keep cool.

It didn't seem natural that a girl would worry so much about a Bible. So when I found hers, I gave it a shake. Out dropped a piece of paper. *Half-past two*, it said.

I didn't know what that meant. I put the paper in the book again and went home. When I got upstairs, Miss Sophia was at my door, waiting for me.

She looked in the Bible and found the note. Her face seemed happy when she read it. Her eyes lit up and she gave me a big hug. She looked awful pretty.

When I got my breath again, I asked her about the note.

"Oh, it's only a bookmark," she said.

## Chapter 15
## A Terrible Feud

I left Miss Sophia and went down to the river. Jack, my slave, followed me. When no one else was around, he said: "Master George, come down to the swamp. I want to show you a snake."

"All right," I said.

We walked for about twenty minutes, to a stretch of land thick with bushes and vines.

"Look right in there," he said. We poked around in the bushes until we came to an open patch. A man lay on the ground, asleep. It was Jim!

I woke him up, hoping to surprise him. He almost cried, he was so glad to see me. But he wasn't surprised. He said that he'd followed me the night our raft was hit by the steamboat.

"I got a little bruised," he said, "and couldn't swim fast. So I figured I'd catch up with you on land. I got scared, though, when I saw all those dogs."

Jim told me how he'd hidden in a field

near the Grangerfords' house. "Early the next morning," he said, "some of the slaves came out and helped. They brought me food every day."

"Why didn't you have them fetch me sooner?" I said.

"I've been busy patching up the raft."

"What raft, Jim?"

"Our old raft."

"You mean it wasn't smashed to bits?"

"Nope, just torn up a bit. But I fixed it good as new."

After a while, I left Jim and went back to the house. Next day, I awoke at dawn. Buck wasn't there. I couldn't find anybody downstairs, either. Out by the woodpile, I saw Jack.

"What's going on?" I said.

"Don't you know, Master George?"

"No."

"Miss Sophia ran off in the night to marry that young Harney Shepherdson."

"Why didn't Buck wake me?"

"The family just found out a half hour

ago," he said. "There wasn't time to lose."

I ran up the river road as fast as I could. I began to hear guns in the distance. When I got to the general store, I hid among the brush. Then I climbed into a tree, out of reach.

Four or five men galloped around on their horses. They cussed and yelled at two boys behind the woodpile. One of them was Buck.

After the men left, I called out to Buck. He was surprised to hear my

voice coming from a tree. He said his father and two brothers had been killed.

"What happened to young Harney and Miss Sophia?" I asked.

"They got across the river."

I was glad to hear they were safe. But Buck said he was disappointed that he hadn't killed Harney. All of a sudden, we heard gunfire. The men had slipped around the woodpile and come in from behind. The boys jumped into the river to escape.

As they swam away, the men stood on the bank, firing their guns. "Kill them! Kill them!" they shouted. These people were crazy. I was tired of so much killing, and wished I'd never come ashore.

I stayed in the tree until it got dark. Some of the men were still in the woods, fighting. I decided to never go near the Grangerford house again. I figured that the note I'd given Miss Sophia had told her when to meet Harney. Maybe if I'd told her father, none of this awful mess would have happened.

When I got out of the tree, I crept along the bank. There were two bodies lying at the edge of the river. I pulled them onto the shore, and covered up their faces. I cried a little when I covered Buck's face. He'd been mighty good to me.

I set out for the swamp. Jim wasn't there, so I ran through the willows to the raft. It was gone! It took me a minute to catch my breath. Then I called out: "Hello!"

A voice about twenty yards away said: "Is that you, Huck? Don't make no noise." It was Jim's voice.

I ran to where he was hiding and got aboard. Jim was so glad to see me, he hugged me.

"Jack thought you'd been shot," Jim said. "I was just about to take off. I'm mighty glad to get you back again."

"Head for the big water as fast as you can," I said. "They'll think I've been killed and floated down the river."

I didn't breathe easier until we were out in the middle of the Mississippi.

By then I was starving. Jim gave me corn bread, pork, cabbage, and greens. While I ate my supper, we talked and had a good time.

I sure was glad to get away from the feuds. And Jim was glad to get away from the swamp. We agreed that there was no home like a raft.

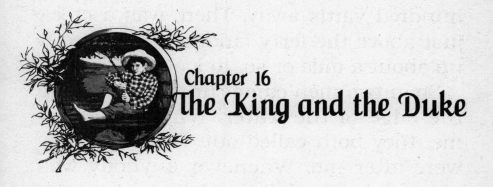

## Chapter 16
# The King and the Duke

Two or three days went by. Sometimes we'd have the river all to ourselves. Once in a while, we'd pass a small village and see a lone candle in a cabin window. Or else we'd hear fiddle music coming from a steamboat.

Mostly we enjoyed the beauty of the river. By day, we'd camp on an island and sleep. We'd go for islands with lots of trees. That way, we could make a fire and cook a hot breakfast without anybody seeing the smoke and getting suspicious.

One morning I found a canoe. So I paddled over to the shore, about two hundred yards away. There was a creek just above the ferry landing. I followed it up about a mile or so, to look for berries.

Soon two men came running out along the edge of the water. When they saw me, they both called out. I thought they were after me. Whenever anybody was after anybody, I figured it was *me*—or Jim—they were after.

But they were being chased by angry villagers—and a pack of dogs. The men wanted to jump right into the canoe. I told them to go out to the end of the path.

"Then get in the water and wade down to me," I said. "That'll throw the dogs off the scent." Once they were aboard, I paddled as quickly as I could back to the raft.

When the men saw Jim, they wanted to know if he was a runaway slave.

"Gosh, no," I said. "Would a runaway

slave run *south*?"

"No," they said, and left it at that.

One of the men was about thirty, and kind of pale. The older one had a bald head and gray whiskers. He wore a crumpled hat, a greasy blue shirt, and ragged blue jeans stuffed into his boot tops. A long-tailed coat with brass buttons was flung over his arm. Both men had fat, ratty-looking bags.

After breakfast we sat around talking. I realized that these two fellows didn't know each other. But they had something in common: They'd both been trying to swindle money from folks who lived along the river.

"Old man," the young one said. "I reckon we might work together. What do you think?"

"I don't see why not," the old man replied. After that, nobody said anything for a while. Then the young one sighed.

"What are you sighin' about?" the old man said.

"To think that my life has come to this."

"Ain't the company good enough for ya?" the old man said.

"Yes, it is. I ain't blaming you, gentlemen. I brought myself down."

"Down from where?"

"Ah, you would not believe me," the young one said. "No one believes the secret of my birth."

"The secret of your birth?"

"Gentlemen, I will reveal it to you. I am a duke!"

Jim stared in amazement. So did I.

"You can't mean it," the old man said.

"Yes. My great-grandfather, eldest son of the Duke of Bridgewater, came to this country in the last century. I am his descendant. And here I sit, ragged, worn, despised. Stuck on a raft."

Jim and I tried to comfort him, but he said it was no use. The only way to make him feel better, he said, was for us to bow when speaking to him, and say, "Your Grace" or "Your Lordship."

When dinner was ready, he asked that we wait on him. So we did. Jim stood around saying, "Will Your Grace have some of this or some of that?"

The duke was pleased by all of the attention. But the old man got quiet. He seemed to have something on his mind.

"Looky here, Bilgewater," he said finally. "I'm sorry for you, but you ain't the only person who has troubles like that."

"No?"

"No, you ain't. I, too, have a secret."

"What do you mean?"

"Bilgewater, can I trust you?" said the old man.

"To the bitter death! Tell me the secret of your being."

"I am the late Dauphin!"

Jim and I couldn't believe our ears. The duke said: "You are the *what*?"

"I am the poor, disappeared Dauphin, Louis the Seventeenth, son of Louis the Sixteenth."

"You?"

"I'm afraid so. You see before you, in blue jeans and misery, the wandering, trampled-on, rightful king of France." He began to cry. Jim and I didn't know what to do. We felt sorry for him, but glad and proud that he was with us.

We tried to comfort him. "It's no use," he said. But, he added, some things would make him feel better. Like us getting down on one knee to speak to him, and saying, "Your Majesty."

He wanted us to wait on him first at meals, which we did. But then the duke got kind of sore.

"Well, Bilgewater," the king said, "we've got to be together on this raft for a long time. So what's the use of being sour? After all, we have plenty of food and an easy life."

The duke agreed, and they shook hands. Jim and I were happy that they'd made up. We didn't want any unfriendliness on the raft.

But it didn't take me long to realize that these liars weren't kings or dukes. They were just frauds. Still, I didn't let on. That way, we wouldn't have any fights or get into trouble. If I never learned anything else from Pap, at least I'd learned one thing: To get along with his kind of people, it's best to let them have their own way.

# Chapter 17
# Royal Nonesuch

$\mathcal{A}$ few nights later, the two Majesties put on a play in a village along the river. The play was called *Royal Nonesuch*. When it ended, the townspeople threw tomatoes at the stage. Then they chased us to the raft. The whole way, the duke clutched a bagful of coins he'd collected.

With some of the money, the king bought himself a new black cape. He looked grand in it.

It wasn't long before the Majesties

eyed another village along the river. They laid out a plan for cheating the people who lived there.

"Whatever Your Majesties decide to do," Jim said, "don't be too long." He didn't like having to hide in the tipi all day. But it couldn't be helped. If folks laid eyes on him, they'd turn him in.

"We'll do our best," the duke said, "to swindle this lovely little Arkansas village as quickly as possible."

Jim cleaned up the canoe for me, and I got my paddle ready. He went back into the tipi while the rest of us headed over to Greenville.

Along the way, the king tugged on his cape and said, "Seein' how I'm dressed, I'd better arrive from some big place, like St. Louis. Head for that steamboat, Huckleberry. We'll come down to the village on that."

The steamboat was stopped about three miles above town, taking on freight. So I headed upstream. Pretty soon, we saw an innocent-looking boy sitting on a log. He swabbed the sweat from his face as we approached.

"Where you bound for?" the king asked, seeing the boy's bags.

"For the steamboat. I'm going to New Orleans."

"Get aboard," the king said. "My servant will help you with your bags." The king looked at me and said, "Adolphus, jump out and help this gentleman."

The young chap was mighty thankful. He said it was tough work toting such bags in warm weather. He asked the king where we were headed.

"We're on our way to see an old friend, a gentleman farmer."

"When I first saw you," the boy said, "I thought you were Mr. Wilks. The whole town's waiting for him. You ain't him?"

"No. My name's Blodgett. Alexander Blodgett. I'm just a poor preacher. Still, I'm sorry that Mr. Wilks hasn't arrived yet. Why is everyone waiting for him?"

"His brother Peter died last night. He's expected from England, to inherit his brother's money and look after his orphaned nieces."

"What's his first name?" the king said.

"Harvey. His brother William is expected, too. William is deaf and mute."

Pretty soon, the king knew what town Harvey was from, who Peter's good friends were, and the names of all three nieces.

"When is the funeral?" the king asked.

"Tomorrow," the boy told him.

When we got near the steamboat, the boy got on, but the king decided not to board, after all. He had me paddle up another mile, to a deserted field. Then he went ashore.

As the duke and I hid the canoe, the king began to talk like an Englishman.

"How are you on being deaf and mute, Bilgewater?" he asked.

The duke said that he had played a deaf and mute person in a theatrical production once. He began to practice some hand signs.

When we got to Greenville, we saw a group of men outside the general store.

"Can any of you gentlemen tell me where Mr. Peter Wilks lives?" the king said. The men looked at each other.

"I'm sorry, sir," one of the men said. "But the best we can do is tell you where he lived yesterday."

The king put his chin on the man's shoulder and started sobbing. "Alas," he

said, "our poor brother is gone! And we never got to see him!"

He turned around and made hand signs to the duke. What a couple of frauds. The townspeople, meanwhile, gathered around and told the king how sorry they were. Whenever they spoke, the king repeated everything to the duke with hand signs.

It was enough to make anyone ashamed of the human race.

## Chapter 18
## Two Frauds

The news spread in minutes. People came running from every doorway. Soon we were in the middle of a mob.

When we got to the Wilks house, the street in front was packed. Mary Jane, the eldest niece, jumped into her Uncle Harvey's arms. The younger girls hugged the duke. Neighbors cried for joy.

We entered the house. The king immediately eyed the coffin standing in the parlor. "Shhh!" everyone said, as the two frauds walked across the room. The king bent over the coffin and began to sob. You could have heard him all the way in New Orleans. The three girls—and everyone else—broke down and cried.

The king thanked the neighbors for coming. Then he sobbed again. The duke made all sorts of signs with his hands. He said, "Goo-goo, goo-goo," like a baby that can't talk.

Mary Jane fetched the letter that her uncle had left behind. She handed it to

the king, who read it aloud. It gave three thousand dollars in gold, and the house, to the girls—and three thousand dollars to Harvey and William.

The money, Wilks's letter said, was hidden in the cellar. So the two frauds went down to get it. They told me to come with them. I shut the cellar door behind us. When they found the bag, they spilled it out on the floor. It wasn't a bad sight—all them yellow coins. The king's eyes shone.

"Why, Biljy," he said. "This sure beats doing *Royal Nonesuch*."

Most anybody would have been satisfied with a pile of gold. But not those two. They had to count it.

"It comes out four hundred and fifteen dollars short," the king said.

"Let's not say anything about it," the duke said. "We'll just make up the difference ourselves." He began to yank yellow coins from his pockets.

"Brilliant," the king said. "Besides, we're going to get it all back."

"I've got another idea," the duke said. "Let's take the money upstairs and give it *all* to the girls."

"A dazzling idea," said the king. "Now they won't suspect us of being frauds."

We went upstairs and the king made another sickening speech.

"Peter would want the girls to have all of the money," he said. "They are poor orphaned lambs." He and the duke

hugged each other, while the duke goo-gooed all over the place.

The king's English accent was pretty bad. One man laughed right in his face. Everyone else was shocked.

"Why, *doctor*!" one of the neighbors said to the man who had laughed. "Ain't you heard the news? This here is Mr. Harvey Wilks."

The king stepped forward and put his hands on the doctor's shoulders. "My poor brother's dear friend," he said. "Doctor Robinson."

"Get your hands off me!" the doctor shouted. "You don't talk like an Englishman! That's the worst imitation of an English accent I ever heard!"

The crowd tried to quiet the doctor. They begged him not to hurt Harvey's feelings. But the doctor kept shouting. "*You*, Peter Wilks's brother?" he said. "You're a fraud, that's what you are!"

The girls hung on the king, crying. The doctor turned to them. "I was your

uncle's friend," he said, "and I am *your* friend. Please listen to me. These men are liars!"

Mary Jane stepped forward. "Here is my answer!" she said. She lifted the bag of money and put it in the king's hands. "Take this six thousand dollars and invest it for me and my sisters, any way you want," she told him.

"Fine," the doctor said, "I wash my hands of this whole matter." He walked out the door, slamming it behind him.

# Chapter 19
# Gold in the Coffin

The neighbors looked stunned. Several of them ran after the doctor, trying to calm him down. The king acted as if nothing had happened.

"Mary Jane," he said, "how are you fixed for spare bedrooms?"

"Please, Uncle Harvey, take *my* room. I'll sleep on a cot in my sisters' room."

"That's awful kind of you," he said. "I *am* weary."

"Let me move my dresses out of the

way," she said, "so you'll have more room."

"Thank you, darling girl, but it's not necessary."

"As you wish, Uncle." Mary Jane had the kindest smile I'd ever seen. She turned to the duke.

"My poor, dear uncle," she said, "you must be exhausted from the journey."

Everyone laughed.

"Oh, Uncle William! I forgot you can't hear! Can you ever forgive me?"

The duke motioned wildly with his

hands, then made himself comfortable in the spare room. I got a cot in the attic.

That night there was a big supper. A bunch of women from the neighborhood helped cook. I stood behind the king's and the duke's chairs and waited on them. Slaves waited on everyone else.

The womenfolk fussed over the biscuits and fried chicken. "How do you get your biscuits to brown so nice?" one said. "Where, for land's sake, did you get these amazin' pickles?" another said.

After supper, I talked with the girls. Mary Jane told the younger two to treat me extra nice.

"Remember," she said. "He's not in his own country, with his own people, so be kind to him."

I felt like a worm. Here I was, letting the old fakes rob her of her money. So I made up my mind that I'd get it back for her. I just had to figure out where it was.

While the king and the duke talked with neighbors, I snuck upstairs to search their rooms. It was awful dark up there. When I heard footsteps, I hid behind Mary Jane's dresses.

"What's wrong?" the king said, as he and the duke entered the room.

The duke shut the door. "I'm worried about that doctor," he said. "I think we should leave in the middle of the night. We could make it across the river before anyone missed us."

"And not sell the rest of the property?" the king said. "Do you expect me to

leave eight or nine thousand dollars' worth of property just lying around?"

"The gold is enough," the duke said.

"No, it ain't," said the king. "Besides, we've got all the fools in town on our side." He turned towards the door.

"Wait," the duke whispered. "I don't think we put the money in a good place."

"I guess you're right," the king said. He fumbled behind one of the dresses, about three feet away from me. I kept as still as I could.

"Here, this is better," the king said. He stuffed the bag beneath the mattress. "When the slaves clean the room, they'll never think to look here."

Before they were halfway down the stairs, I was up in my cubby with the gold coins. I decided to hide them outside. I got into bed with my clothes on, waiting for everyone to go to sleep.

When the house was finally quiet, I climbed down the ladder. It was pitch dark. At the bottom of the stairs, I stubbed my toe.

The parlor door was open. There was a candle on the table. I could see the coffin in the middle of the room. It gave me the creeps.

I heard footsteps. The only place to hide the money was in the coffin. I tucked it under the lid and hid behind the door.

Mary Jane walked into the room, but she didn't see me. She went over to the coffin, knelt down, and began to cry. I slid out behind her and up to bed.

## Chapter 20
## A Narrow Escape

In the morning, they buried Peter Wilks. But not before the king speechified about his "poor brother that lies yonder." I didn't know if anyone had found the gold or if it was still in the coffin.

That evening, the king visited all the neighbors. He told them that he and his brother had to hurry home to England, to take care of an urgent matter. He said that they would have to settle Peter Wilks's estate right away. Everyone said that they were sorry to see the two brothers leave.

The next day, the king sold off the slaves. He sold two boys up the river to Memphis, and their mother down the river to New Orleans. Mary Jane and the slaves wept with grief.

Even some of the townspeople were angry. But the king went ahead with his plans. He scheduled an auction for the next afternoon. Mary Jane said that she and her sisters would go visit friends in the country, so as not to be in the way. I felt awful sad as the girls hurried out the door with the few belongings left to them.

In the morning, the king and the duke came up to my cubby. I saw by their eyes that there was trouble.

"Was you in my room the other night?" the king said.

"No, Your Majesty."

"I don't want any lies."

"Honest. I haven't been in there since Mary Jane first showed it to you."

"Did you see anybody else go in there?"

Here was my chance. "Just some slaves," I said.

The king and the duke looked at each other. "When?"

"The morning of the funeral."

"How did they act?"

"I just thought they were cleaning up," I said, looking all innocent. "Why? Is something wrong?"

"None of your business!" the king snarled. Then he turned to the duke: "We'll just have to keep this to ourselves."

"I told you we should have taken the money and cleared out!" the duke said.

That afternoon they held the auction in the public square. Everything Peter Wilks had ever owned was put up for sale. The king slid coins into the lining of his cape, while the duke goo-gooed.

The last item for sale was a graveyard lot. While the king sold that, a steamboat landed. Soon a crowd came into the square, whooping and carrying on.

"*These* two gentlemen," someone shouted, "also claim to be the Wilks brothers."

Lots of folks gathered around the king, to let him know they were on his side. The real Harvey Wilks looked puzzled. But soon he began to speak—with a *real* English accent.

"I am Harvey Wilks, Peter's brother," he said. "This is my brother William. He can neither hear nor speak. We *are* who we say we are."

"Prove it!" someone in the crowd shouted.

"I will prove it in a day or two, when I get our baggage. Until then, I won't say anything more."

"Lost their baggage!" said the king. "That's a good one!"

Everybody laughed, except for a few people.

"Wait a moment," the real Harvey said. "I've thought of something. I can tell you

what was tattooed on my brother's breast."

By now the doctor, a lawyer, and some other people had gathered around.

"Tell us," the lawyer said to the king. "What mark is on Peter Wilks's breast?"

The king looked shaken. I could see that he was stumped. "A thin blue arrow," he said, finally.

"Ahhh!" the crowd said, relieved.

The lawyer turned to the real Harvey.

"What was the mark on Peter Wilks's breast?" he said.

"A small *P* and a small *W*. His initials."

The lawyer turned to the undertakers. "Tell us, gentlemen, what marks did *you* see?"

"We never saw any marks at all," the men said. By now the crowd was really worked up.

"They're all frauds!" they shouted.

"Let 'em all drown!"

"Gentlemen, please," said the lawyer.

"There's only one way to resolve this. We'll go and dig up the corpse."

"Hooray!" everyone shouted.

Then the lawyer said: "Collar these four men and the boy, and bring them along, too!"

"If we don't find the marks," someone yelled. "We'll lynch 'em!"

They gripped us all and marched us to the graveyard. The folks in back nearly trampled us. I'd never been so scared.

As we neared the graveyard, the sky

darkened. Wind shook the leaves and lightning began to flicker. We soon got to Peter Wilks's grave. There were lots of shovels, but no one had brought a lantern. People started digging anyway, by the flickers of lightning.

A heavy rain began to fall, and the thunder boomed. Shovelsful of dirt sailed up out of the grave.

At last they reached the coffin and began to unscrew the lid. Everyone shoved in closer. The guy clutching my wrist got so excited he nearly twisted my arm off.

All of a sudden, lightning lit up the sky. "By jingo," someone sang out, "there's a bag of gold on his breast!"

Everyone let out a whoop. In the excitement, the guy holding me let go. He busted his way forward, to get a look.

I took off before anyone noticed. As I ran past the Wilks house, my heart swelled up a little, because of Mary Jane. She was the best girl I'd ever known.

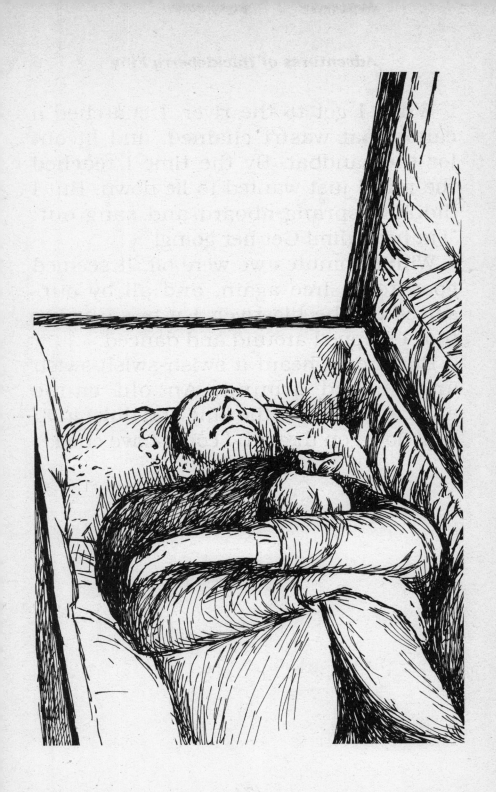

When I got to the river, I snatched a canoe that wasn't chained, and lit out for the sandbar. By the time I reached the raft, I just wanted to lie down. But I didn't. I sprang aboard and sang out: "I'm here, Jim! Get her going!"

Within minutes we were off. It seemed good to be free again, and all by ourselves on the big river. I was so happy that I skipped around and danced.

But then I heard a swish-swish-swish and turned around. An old canoe approached—with the king and duke in it! I fell down on the raft. I could have cried.

## Chapter 21
## On the Farm

**W**hen they got aboard, the king shook me by the collar.

"Tryin' to give us the slip, was ya?"

"No, Your Majesty," I said. "We weren't. Honest."

The king accused me of hiding the gold in Peter Wilks's coffin. But the duke told him to lay off. Then they went into the tipi and stewed for a while.

We had to stay on the river for three days, to get as far from Greenville as

possible. The duke and the king hardly spoke. But the duke soon got a look in his eyes. I knew it meant trouble. He began to talk to the king in low, confidential tones.

The next day, we landed near a town called Pikesville. Jim stayed in the tipi, while we went ashore. The king told the duke and me to wait in the woods. He set off for Pikesville, to see if anyone had heard of *Royal Nonesuch*.

The duke and I waited for hours. Then we went into town. We found the king lecturing some townfolk about the dangers of drinking. He was drunker than Pap had ever been—if that's possible.

While the duke lit into him, I took off. I raced back to the raft.

"Set her loose, Jim!" I called. "We're free of them!"

But Jim was gone. I shouted and shouted. No answer. I ran into the woods, looking every which way. Nothing.

I sat down and cried. But I couldn't sit still for long. I got onto the road, trying to decide what to do. Pretty soon, a boy came along.

"Have you seen any slaves wanderin' near here?" I said.

"Yes, I seen a runaway."

"Whereabouts?"

"Well, they captured him and took him to the Phelps farm."

"Who nailed him?" I asked.

"A stranger. He sold the slave to Mr. Phelps for forty dollars. Said he had to go up the river, and couldn't wait for the rightful owner."

"By any chance, did the stranger mention a play called *Royal Nonesuch*?" I asked.

"Why, yes. Do you know him?"

"His reputation is fairly large," I said.

So the king had sold Jim! After all we'd done for the scoundrel! I'd fix the evil fraud.

"Tell the villagers," I said, "to ask

about *Royal Nonesuch* a few towns up the river. They'll find out who that stranger is."

"I'll tell my pa."

"First, could you show me the way to the Phelps farm? I'd like to see the captured runaway."

He gave me directions and I set off. Along the way I got to thinking: If Jim had to be a slave again, at least he should be at home, where his family was.

I'd write to Tom Sawyer. *He* could tell

Miss Watson about Jim. I reckoned she was no longer speaking to me.

But I soon gave up that idea. Everyone in town would despise Jim for running away. They'd hate me, too, because I'd helped a slave try to get his freedom.

There was only one solution: I had to free Jim. Maybe I was a bad boy, headed for the place down below. But that's what my conscience told me to do. I ran the rest of the way.

At the Phelps farm, a woman stood by the fence, as if she were waiting for me. Two small children peered out from behind her dress.

"Hello there," she said. "I thought the steamboat had gotten lost."

I had to figure out who I was supposed to be, and where I was coming from.

"The boat had engine trouble," I said, without mentioning if I'd come from up north or down south. I needed to get a few more clues from her.

"Come over here and give your Aunt

Sally a big hug, Tom Sawyer," she said. "I'm mighty glad to see you."

Tom Sawyer? Phew. I could easily fake being him. But if he showed up all of a sudden, I'd be in trouble. I gave Aunt Sally a hug, then said I had to go fetch my bags at the landing.

On the way back to town, I ran into Tom. His mouth opened wide in amazement when he saw me.

"I ain't ever done you no harm," he said.

"Why are you comin' back to haunt me?"

"I ain't a ghost, Tom," I said. "Here, touch my arm."

That satisfied him. I explained how I'd tricked everyone back home into thinking that I'd been murdered. Then I told him about Aunt Sally.

"That's easy," he said. "We'll pretend that you're Sid, my half-brother. She's never met him, either."

"Okay," I said. "But there's one more

thing I have to tell you." I took a deep breath. "I'm here to steal someone out of slavery. Ol' Miss Watson's Jim."

"Jim? How did *that* happen?"

I thought for sure Tom would hate me now. But he didn't. "I'll *help* you steal him!" he said cheerfully.

We put our heads together for a long while. Then we headed back to the Phelps's to rescue Jim. If there's one thing you should know about Tom Sawyer, it's this: In addition to liking a good adventure, he's got lots of style.

## Epilogue
# A Free Man

Tom has *so* much style, it would take another book to tell you how we freed Jim. Tom got all fancy with his escape plans. Before I knew it, half the men in the village were chasing us with guns. Tom even got shot in the leg.

Right then, Jim could have lit out on the raft and saved himself. But he risked his freedom to save Tom's life. He stayed with Tom until I got back with a doctor.

Jim got recaptured. But when Aunt Sally and the men learned that he had helped save Tom, they made a big fuss over him. We had him out of chains in no time. Then we heard some big news: Jim was a free man—by law. Ol' Miss Watson had died two months before—and she'd set him free in her will.

Tom said that the three of us should slide out of there right away. We could celebrate by having some howling-good adventures together. I thought it was a

good idea. But I told him I was broke. I figured Pap had been back to get my money from Judge Thatcher.

"Well, he hasn't," Tom said.

Then Jim said, "Don't worry. He ain't comin' back, Huck."

"How do you know?"

"Never you mind," Jim said.

But I kept at him until he gave in. "Do you remember that house," he said, "that was floatin' down the river? And that dead man whose face I covered up,

and told you not to look? Well, that man was your pap."

So I was free, too. I went back to St. Petersburg and got my money. Tom, who's mending fine, wears the bullet that wounded him on a chain around his neck. As for the king and the duke, they got tarred and feathered after folks learned about *Royal Nonesuch*.

There ain't nothin' more to write about. And I'm glad of it. If I'd known what trouble it was to make a book, I never would've tackled it in the first place.

I guess I'll light out for Injun Territory ahead of the others. Aunt Sally wants to adopt me and civilize me, and I can't stand it. I've been there before.

The End

# ABOUT THE AUTHOR

**SAMUEL LANGHORNE CLEMENS** was born in Florida, Missouri, in 1835. He left home in 1853 and tried several different careers.

Clemens first used the pseudonym "Mark Twain" in 1863, as his signature on a humorous letter. Little did he know then how famous that name would make him.

He published his first novel-length book in 1869, followed by many others, including *The Adventures of Tom Sawyer*, *The Prince and the Pauper*, and *A Connecticut Yankee in King Arthur's Court*. Some of the events recorded in *Adventures of Huckleberry Finn*, first published in 1884, are said to be an accurate account of the author's own adventurous childhood antics.

Clemens died in 1910, leaving great gifts for the world—and a name that will live forever.

# The Young Collector's
# Illustrated Classics

Adventures of Huckleberry Finn
The Adventures of Robin Hood
The Adventures of Tom Sawyer
Anne of Green Gables
Black Beauty
Call of the Wild
Dracula
Frankenstein
Gulliver's Travels
Heidi
The Hunchback of Notre Dame
A Little Princess
Little Women
Moby Dick
Oliver Twist
Peter Pan
The Prince and the Pauper
The Secret Garden
The Strange Case of Dr. Jekyll and Mr. Hyde
Swiss Family Robinson
The Time Machine
Treasure Island
20,000 Leagues Under the Sea
White Fang

These Illustrated Classics are available for special
and educational sales from:
## www.kidsbooks.com

Kidsbooks, Inc.
3535 West Peterson Avenue
Chicago, IL 60659
(800) 515-5437